THIS CANDLEWICK BOOK BELONGS TO:

_____

_____

_____

_____

For Lon, who loves umbrellas,
and for Ivy and Ian, the Florida cousins

A. H.

For Natalie and Sophie Lou,
my granddaughters

J. B.

Text copyright © 1995 by Amy Hest
Illustrations copyright © 1995 by Jill Barton

First U.S. paperback edition 1999

The Library of Congress has cataloged the hardcover edition as follows:

Hest, Amy, date.
In the rain with Baby Duck / Amy Hest / illustrated by Jill Barton.—1st ed.
Summary: Although her parents love walking in the rain, Baby Duck does
not—until Grampa shares a secret with her.
ISBN 978-1-56402-532-6 (hardcover)
[1. Rain and rainfall—Fiction. 2. Ducks—Fiction.
3. Grandfathers—Fiction.] I. Barton, Jill, ill. II. Title.
PZ7.H4375In   1995
[E]—dc20   94-48929
ISBN 978-0-7636-0697-8 (paperback)

18 19 20 21 22 APS 16 15 14 13

Printed in Humen, Dongguan, China

This book was typeset in OPTI Lucius Ad Bold.
The illustrations were done in pencil and watercolor.

Candlewick Press
99 Dover Street
Somerville, Massachusetts 02144

visit us at www.candlewick.com

In the Rain
with
Baby Duck

Amy Hest

illustrated by **Jill Barton**

CANDLEWICK PRESS

Pit-pat.

Pit-a-pat.

Pit-a-pit-a-pat.

Oh, the rain came down.

It poured and poured.

Baby Duck was mad.

She did not like walking in the rain.

But it was Pancake Sunday, a Duck family tradition, and Baby loved pancakes.

And she loved Grampa, who was waiting on the other side of town.

Pit-pat. Pit-a-pat. Pit-a-pit-a-pat.

"Follow us! Step lively!" Mr. and Mrs.
Duck left the house arm in arm.

"Wet feet," wailed Baby.

"Don't dally, dear.
Don't drag behind,"
called Mr. Duck.

"Wet face," pouted Baby. "Water in my eyes."

Mrs. Duck pranced along. "See how

the rain rolls off your back!"

"Mud," muttered Baby.

"Mud, mud, mud."

"Don't dawdle, dear! Don't lag behind!"

Mr. and Mrs. Duck skipped ahead.

They waddled. They shimmied.

They hopped in all the puddles.

Baby dawdled. She dallied and

pouted and dragged behind.

She sang a little song.

"I do not like the rain one bit

Splashing down my neck.

Baby feathers soaking wet,

I do not like this mean old day."

"Are you singing?" called Mr. and Mrs. Duck.

"What a fine thing to do in the rain!"

Baby stopped singing.

Grampa was waiting at the front door.

He put his arm around Baby.

"Wet feet?" he asked.

"Yes," Baby said.

"Wet face?"

Grampa asked.

"Yes," Baby said.

"Mud?" Grampa asked.

"Yes," Baby said. "Mud, mud, mud."

"I'm afraid the rain makes Baby cranky,"
clucked Mr. Duck.

"I've never heard of a duck who doesn't
like rain," worried Mrs. Duck.

"Is that a fact?" Grampa kissed Baby's cheeks.

Grampa took Baby's hand.

"Come with me, Baby."

They went upstairs to the attic.

"We are looking for a tall green bag," Grampa said.

Finally they found it.

Inside was a beautiful red umbrella.

There were matching boots, too.

"These used to be your mother's," Grampa whispered. "A long time ago, she was a baby duck who did not like rain."

Baby opened the umbrella.

The boots were just the right size.

Baby and Grampa marched downstairs.

"My boots!" cried Mrs. Duck. "And my bunny umbrella!"

"No, mine!" said Baby.

"You look lovely," said Mrs. Duck.

Mr. Duck put a platter of pancakes on the table.

After that, Baby and Grampa went outside.

Pit-pat. Pit-a-pat. Pit-a-pit-a-pat.

Oh, the rain came down.

It poured and poured.

Baby Duck and Grampa

walked arm in arm

in the rain.

They

waddled.

They
shimmied.

They hopped in all
the puddles.

And Baby Duck sang a new song.

"I really like the rain a lot
Splashing my umbrella.
Big red boots on baby feet,
I really love this rainy day."

AMY HEST loves walking in the rain. "Good weather can be such a bore," she says. She is the author of numerous books for children, including the Baby Duck series; *Little Chick* and *Kiss Good Night,* both illustrated by Anita Jeram; *When Jessie Came Across the Sea,* illustrated by P.J. Lynch; and *Remembering Mrs. Rossi,* illustrated by Heather Maione. Amy Hest lives in New York City.

JILL BARTON says that the character of Grampa in the Baby Duck books is very much like her own grandfather, who "always took little people's problems very seriously and kindly." Jill Barton is the illustrator of many picture books, including *Rattletrap Car* by Phyllis Root; *Lady Lollipop* by Dick King-Smith; and *It's Quacking Time!* and *The Pig in the Pond,* both by Martin Waddell.